Can't Me!

Timothy a Ciraolo

WALKER BOOKS
AND SUBSIDIARIES
LONDON · BOSTON · SYDNEY · AUCKLAND

Once there was Jake,
the fastest mouse in the world.

Here he is!

OH NO – he's gone!

Quick! After him!

Ah, there he is!

Look how far he's got
in no time flat!

Jake was far too fast for Old Tom Cat.
All Tom wanted was a sweet young mouse
to eat ... but no such luck.

Tom tied himself in knots just trying to catch Jake.

His tummy rumbled. He got thinner and thinner.

"Can't catch me!" sang Jake.
"I'm the fastest mouse in the world!"

And he ran out of the garden and into the fields.

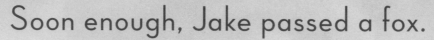

Soon enough, Jake passed a fox.

"Where are you going, you tasty young mouse?"
asked the fox. "I'd like to eat you up."

"I was too fast for Old Tom Cat
and I'll be too fast for you," said Jake.

"We'll see about that!"
barked the fox.

"Can't catch me!"

sang Jake.

"I'm the fastest mouse
in the world."

The fox ran and ran.
It scampered and scurried
but it didn't have a hope,
it couldn't catch Jake.

Jake ran out of the fields,
and into a wood.
Soon enough,
he passed a wolf.

"Where are you going,
you juicy young mouse?"
asked the wolf.
"I'd like to eat you up."

"I was too fast for Old Tom Cat,
too fast for the fox and I'll be
too fast for you," said Jake.

"We'll see about that!"
growled the wolf.

"Can't catch me!" sang Jake.
"I'm the fastest mouse in the world!"

The wolf ran and ran.
It sprinted and sprang but it didn't have
a hope, it couldn't catch Jake.

Jake ran out of the woods and up into
the hills. Soon enough, he passed a bear.
"Where are you going, you scrummy
young mouse?" asked the bear.
"I'd like to eat you up."

"I was too fast for Old Tom Cat
and the fox AND the wolf
and I'll be too fast for you,"
said Jake.

"We'll see about that!"
roared the bear.

"Can't catch me,"

sang Jake.

"I'm the fastest mouse
in the world!"

The bear ran and ran ...
it lunged and leapt ...

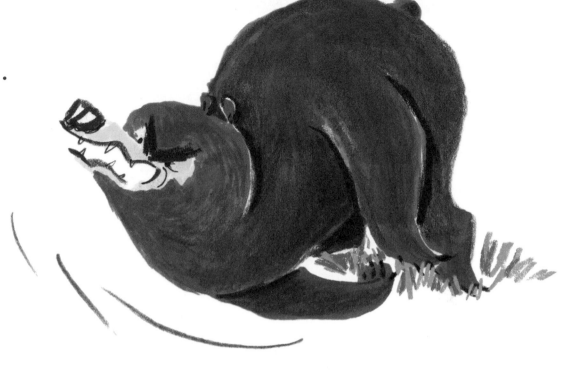

but it didn't have a hope,
it couldn't catch Jake.

Jake ran and ran around
the world – Yippee! –

until he ended up
right back where
he started.

"Where have you been?" Old Tom croaked.

"I ran and ran around the world," said Jake.

"I can't hear you," said Old Tom.

"I'm so weak. Come closer!"

"I was too fast for the bear, too fast for the wolf, too fast for the fox," said Jake.
"Come a little closer," said Old Tom.
"I haven't eaten in such a looooong time."

"And I'm too fast for YOU,"
said Jake.

"Closer still," said Old Tom Cat.

"I'm just a bag of bones."

"Can't catch me!" sang Jake. "I'm—"

"Delicious,"
said Old Tom Cat.

To David and John, with love ~T.K.

To Anna ~S.C.

First published 2017 by Walker Books Ltd
87 Vauxhall Walk, London SE11 5HJ

This edition published 2018

2 4 6 8 10 9 7 5 3 1

Text © 2017 Timothy Knapman • Illustrations © 2017 Simona Ciraolo

The right of Timothy Knapman and Simona Ciraolo to be identified as author and illustrator respectively
of this work has been asserted by them in accordance with the Copyright, Designs and Patents Act 1988

This book has been typeset in Neutraface Display Medium Alt

Printed in China

British Library Cataloguing in Publication Data: a catalogue record for this book is available from the British Library

ISBN 978-1-4063-7839-9

www.walker.co.uk